# facebook addiction

# facebook addiction

The Life & Times of Social Networking Addicts

**Nnamdi Godson Osuagwu**

**ice cream melts publishing**

Facebook Addiction
The Life & Times of Social Networking Addicts
All Rights Reserved.
Copyright © 2009 Nnamdi Godson Osuagwu
v2.0

Copyedit by Sonia Butler Canzater

Published by Ice Cream Melts Publishing
info@icecreammelts.com

ISBN : 978-0-9797480-3-5

PRINTED IN THE UNITED STATES OF AMERICA

# table of contents

nnamdi g. osuagwu      ix

toni lane      1

jeff frake      7

robert blage      13

ellen kane      17

jennifer towers      21

johnny rocket      25

michael sandelli      31

natasha harrington      35

august stone      41

fluffy      45

carrie - tyler's mom      49

social networking addiction guide      53

social networking anonymous 12 steps      61

basic structure of social networking anonymous    63

social networking addiction childhood theory    65

news articles    69

conclusion    83

social networking terms and definitions    87

references    91

keep in touch    95

acknowledgements    97

# Sign Up
# It's Free and Anyone Can Join

Full Name: 

Your Email: 

New Password: 

Next >

# introduction

nnamdi g. osuagwu

Hi, my name is Nnamdi Osuagwu and I'm a Social Networking Addict!! There, I said it. That statement, though simple, takes most social networking addicts a lifetime to say. The first step to taking control of your *Social Networking Addiction* is admitting that you have a problem. I have been battling my Social Networking Addiction for two years and finally got control of the situation a few months ago. I can now say that I've been Social Network-free for 60 days. Although short in time, in the eyes of a Social Networker this is a lifetime; a lifetime of not being involved in the lives of your friends, not updating your status, not sharing links to cool stuff on the internet, not updating your pictures, not tagging friends in photos, not seeing who tagged you in photos. It is torture. Complete and insane torture.

Your world is so bland. You watch TV wondering what others in your network think about what you just watched. You go out and the day just seems so dull. Everything that is worth sharing, you can't. You see something interesting on the street and take a picture of it, but you can't upload it to your profile. There is no one to comment on your pictures or random thoughts. Another social networking addict once asked me, "How can you stay clean?" I replied, "One minute at a time brother, just one minute at a time." That is what it is all about. Taking it one minute at a time.

You have to leave the house. Staying home is unbearable. Just you and the laptop. I even contemplated discontinuing my Internet Service Provider. But then there is the Blackberry Facebook application. There are many social networking applications, but Facebook is the most addictive. Some use Myspace, Flickr, Bebo, Twitter, etc., but Facebook is the heroin of social networking. It is the most difficult social networking site to kick. There is a deeper connection to your network than Myspace. Myspace has a bunch of strangers who can be your friends, but Facebook has everyone that you knew in school. It traces back to elementary and all the way to post-graduate studies. And then there are those status updates. I could easily update my status 15 to 20 times in a 24 hour time period. Social Networking Addicts call it "SNEAKING." When you are SNEAKING, you are constantly on status update and message posting mode. I mean, you are updating your status, commenting on other people's status, commenting on pictures, leaving wall posts, etc. You are all over the place. I know other addicts who SNEAKED for 24 hours straight on Redbull and coffee. They were going for it. They were really taking it there!

Just talking about it gives me goose bumps. Then comes the crash. You stop taking phone calls. If someone wants to communicate with you, then they have to leave a wall post on your profile page. You don't even answer emails anymore. Strictly wall posts and no behind-the-scenes messages. Everyone must see everything. You become despondent around your friends and family. You don't want visitors, strictly more friend requests. You stop going out. You are strictly online. You seclude yourself in your house. You stop going to work. You only go out to get food and come right back home. You keep your Blackberry, aka "Crackberry," close by just in case you have to go to the bathroom. You just want to be connected. It is a constant need to be on. Then something happens to your ISP. Verizon goes down in the neighborhood and you are getting bad reception on your cell phone device.

That is when it happens. You are totally frantic. You call Verizon, desperately asking them to help you. They explain that your neighborhood is experiencing issues with DSL service. You start the conversation off calmly, but then you get irate. You threaten to switch providers. You ask to speak to a manager. You tell the person at the call center that you want to speak to someone in America. You go totally ballistic. You then hang up the phone. You try to use your Blackberry, but your wireless connection is down. You can't think. You start thinking that the world is against you, and perhaps it may even be coming to an end. You think that there is another 9/11 going on right outside your apartment! You run outside for some air, thinking that everything outside is at a screeching halt. When you get outside you notice that it is the middle of the day in Manhattan; everyone and everything are all perfectly fine. Cabs are running, people are on the street laughing and talking. Stores are open and conducting business. The street vendors are selling sodas and bagels. The weather is in the mid 70s. You thought it was still winter. All of the above happened to me, and that is when I realized that I'm a Social Networking Addict. That is the day that I took control of my life.

Getting control was not easy. Who do I turn to? Where do I go? Is this a serious problem? These are the questions that Social Networking Addicts like myself are faced with when we realize we have a problem and then try to stop. A lot of us seek ways to wean off of the Social Network. We will go to places where there is no Internet service. Yes, this is the oldest trick in the book, but how long can you stay in some remote dead cell place without your laptop? I tried that initially and eventually had to come home. I remember driving aimlessly until I found a dead zone. Then I just stopped and waited. It was totally pointless and an act of desperation. I eventually came home and jumped right back on my laptop.

On another occasion, I tried to pack up my laptop. Yes, this works until actual work has to be done. A client called and needed me to work on a website. Then the laptop came out. I, of course, tried to focus on the project, but then started to browse the Internet. I typed in *www.facebook.com* and logged in. I told myself, "I will only spend five minutes, max." Three hours later, I was SNEAKING again. I finally caught myself after eight hours.

Another famous tactic is the old "I'm just going to delete my profile" routine. This is one of the bravest things a Social Networking Addict can do. It is like going cold turkey. It can be a totally devastating experience. You are cut off from all of your friends. You are no longer there. It is like you don't exist. All pictures, comments, tags, and wall posts are GONE! That is it, you are no one, and you have been eradicated from existence. This is what I did and it was insane. Can you recall Jamie Foxx in the Ray Charles movie when he was kicking heroin and decided to go cold turkey in the hospital? This is a similar process to a Social Networking Addict.

I would wake up in the middle of the night, thinking

that someone left me an urgent comment. I would check my email messages, and wonder why I didn't receive any Facebook notifications. Not a single wall post comment, event notification or even a message from someone asking me to join a group. That is when it hit me. I have just deleted my Facebook account. It is such an emotional experience, but for extreme cases, this is a possible solution.

It is important to note that all addicts think that every comment is urgent. In reality, comments are not urgent at all. They are mere checkups from mostly casual acquaintances who want to say "Hi," but they don't want real interaction in your life. Maybe a couple of back and forth comments. Perhaps a response to an interesting or philosophical status. Addicts really value these friendships and think that these people are an integral part of their lives. They take all of their comments, wall posts, status updates, etc. extremely seriously. If this person dared not comment or log in because of a real-life issue like, I don't know, WORK or VACATION, then they should have posted it to let everyone know that they won't be online. Addicts are quite delusional about relationships.

Social Networking Addicts place a higher value on their online community than they do their offline community, or the people they see in person. It is quite common for an addict to forget birthdays and anniversaries. Their main excuse would be that they did not get a Facebook or Myspace reminder. Their entire world revolves around their social networking community.

In summary, here are some signs of a Social Networking Addict:

1.  Reclusiveness - They tend to isolate themselves in their homes. In severe cases they would stop taking phone calls.
2.  Forgetfulness - They tend to forget things that don't pertain to their social network, i.e. birthdays of people not in their social network.
3.  **SNEAKING** - This is constant social networking activity for extended periods of time. The highest clocked case of SNEAKING was from a 23-year-old man who stayed "LIVE" for 23 hours and had over 10,000 updates, wall post, comments, and uploads combined. He was really going for it.
4.  Losing track of time while SNEAKING.

Since this epidemic is relatively new, there are constantly new signs being discovered. In my case, I went cold turkey and got control of my habit, but millions of people suffer from Social Networking Addiction and have nowhere to turn. Due to this issue I formed *Social Networking Anonymous* or *S.N.A.* and started a community on **www. SocialNetworkingAddiction.com**. The website is a place where people who suffer from Social Networking Addiction can get together and blog or vlog through their addiction. We provide a support group and forum where people can discuss their addiction openly without judgment. I serve as the host and assist in helping the many who come to our site work through their social networking addiction.

There were initial concerns about forming an online group to help people who suffer from an online social networking addiction. Some compared it to holding an Alcoholics Anonymous meeting in a bar. All of these concerns were seriously considered, but we have found that our fellow members find it easier to communicate in a familiar environment. The goal was never to completely stop our online social networking usage, but to get control and share our issues with people who face a similar affliction. Some of us don't necessarily want to go "cold turkey;" we just want to figure out ways to control it. Currently, this community has been the most efficient forum for doing so and it allows people from different parts of the world to help each other through their addiction.

In the following chapters you will hear from members who have agreed to talk openly about their addiction and how it affected their lives. They agreed to participate in this book to serve as a testimony for other Social Networking Addicts that have not yet come forward or who feel that they are alone.

Social Networking Anonymous can be accessed through www.SocialNetworkingAddiction.com and is easy to join, but there are some basic rules:

1. Everything that is discussed unless otherwise stated is confidential.
2. Members can not solicit other members to join their social network. If members are currently "social network friends" then this rule is voided.

Members who violate the above rules are excused from the group. We collectively decided that the many outweigh the one. We have not had any real incidents since the group has started. When Social Networking Addicts get to this point, they are ready for a change in their lives. They know how hard it is to live as Social Networking Addicts and tend to just drop out of the group on their own free will before becoming a detriment to others.

A complete guide to Social Networking Addiction and S.N.A. can be found at the end of this book.

# chapter 1

toni lane

## 2 | facebook addiction

**Real Name: Toni Lane**
**Social Network Name: Toni Lane**

My name is Toni and I'm a Social Networking Addict. I'm a single woman with a career as a social worker. Everything was perfectly normal in my life. I would go to work, come home, watch my TV shows and do the whole thing all over again the next day. Maybe every once in a while, I'd go to the gym or something. I might see the girlfriends during the week. I also dated occasionally. On weekends I would veg out, clean, buy groceries, go to see some of my friends, or maybe see a new movie.

I didn't even know about social networking. I would just use the computer to check emails. One day I got an email from an old college friend asking me to join Facebook. I ignored the email for a while, but one night, I decided to click the link. I was asked to fill in answers to questions about myself. It was basic stuff like the school I went to, where I was from, my occupation, etc.

After I finished, I started to see so many people from my past come up as "Friend Suggestions" (a Facebook function). There was Alice Jones, my best friend in junior high; Keith Robinson, my high school crush; and John Simmons, my next door neighbor. I also saw Bo, Robert, Elaine, Mya and many others. The list just went on and on.

The friends kept piling on. We started chatting through Wall Post and commenting on each others' Status. It became my new pastime. I would now come home looking forward to what I missed during the day. How was Robert feeling? What philosophical comment did Bo post? What new friend requests did I have waiting for me?

I started with a handful of offline friends and ended up with over 300 online Social Networking friends. It was amazing. I was so involved in most of their lives. They would post so much information, which made it easy to keep track of everyone and everything. As much as I was involved, I felt that I was losing touch when I would go to work. My job blocked most of the popular social networking sites like Facebook, Myspace and Bebo.

I noticed one day, on a News Feed, that a friend added the Facebook application to their Blackberry Mobile Device. I had a regular no frills cell phone at the time, but now needed a Blackberry immediately. Anything that would allow me more Facebook time. Once my carrier upgraded my phone to the Blackberry, I immediately added the Facebook application to my phone. I was now on 24/7.

I think that was the major turning point. It was almost too much accessibility. I noticed myself SNEAKING at work. SNEAKING while at the grocery store. SNEAKING while at the doctor's office. SNEAKING while driving, which is very dangerous. It was getting to the point where people were constantly noticing me on my Blackberry. I just couldn't help myself.

There were times at work that I would go into the bathroom just to SNEAK. I would lock myself in a stall, post comments, update my status messages, and scan the walls of my friends. I would totally lose track of time. I once spent 5 hours in the bathroom after lunch just SNEAKING. I only realized that it was time to go because a friend's wall post mentioned that she was now leaving work. I thought to myself, she is lucky to be leaving work so early. When I looked at my watch it was 7pm! I was shocked and quickly left the bathroom. I proceeded to gather my belongings from my desk and headed home. On the way home I couldn't believe that I spent five hours in the bathroom. It was seriously bothering me how much time had passed. As soon as I got home I hopped on my computer and logged onto Facebook. I then spent all night SNEAKING. When I woke up in front of my computer the next morning, I realized I had a problem.

At this point I didn't know where to turn for help. I thought that I could fight this issue on my own. I immediately uninstalled the Facebook application from my Blackberry and unplugged my computer. That day was like torture. While at work I kept thinking about Facebook and what my friends were up to. It was like being in another world. All I could think about was Facebook. Colleagues would be talking and I would just give blank stares. I couldn't concentrate. I felt so depressed and out of it. I made it through work, but rushed home, plugged in the computer and logged back onto Facebook. It was just too much time being away. I then SNEAKED all night. I was in a cheerful mood the next morning, but also sad that I couldn't stop myself from being online.

I then decided that I needed help, but couldn't for the life of me think where to go or who to turn to. It was not like a serious problem, you know, like drugs or alcohol. That following night, while logged onto Facebook, I started to research on Google in another browser window. I discovered tons of people addicted to Facebook. It was both scary and reassuring that I was not alone. I started to read countless stories and really thought that I needed help like ASAP.

Through further research, I came across a web-site, www.SocialNetworkingAddiction.com. It was a site that was geared towards helping people in my situation. It was anonymous, which was good, and everyone seemed genuine. The meetings were held online, over conference calls or sometimes at offline locations. Also, anyone and everyone can sign up. Even though it was anonymous you could choose to use your real name, but under no circumstances could you solicit friends from the group. I guess it's like bringing alcohol to an A.A. meeting.

It took me about 5 meetings and hearing the sto-ries of others to realize that I have the strength to go OFFLINE. I think it was the story of one lady, Carrie, whose son suffered a terrible accident while she was SNEAKING. That brought a lot of us Social Networking Addicts to tears. Over the conference call, I heard the sad voices. It was one of the worst cases that I have ever heard and even though I didn't have any children, I didn't want that to be me.

I'm officially 10 days OFFLINE, or Social Networking-Free. It feels amazing! I'm tempted every day to log on, but always think about Carrie and stop myself. We have had many discussions about when to go on-line vs. staying offline. Going online is not necessarily bad, if you can control it. It is all about control and not letting the social networking website take control of your life. It seems to be all relative when an addict gets that control. Some get it in 3 days, others never get it. I guess the true test is going back online.

# chapter 2

**jeff frake**

**Real Name: Jeff Frake**

**Social Network Name: Jeff Frake**

My name is Jeff and I'm a Social Networking Addict. I started on Myspace. I didn't want a page, but everyone was convincing me to get one. I finally cracked and got a page. I was 25 at the time and just started a new job as an assistant buyer for Ross Stores (a clothing store). The job was pretty demanding and I basically had to manage the tasks that the buyer, my boss, assigned to me. There were 2 assistants at the time. So back to Myspace. I set up a page and added some music. I then started to get a whole bunch of friend requests from people I didn't know. It was cool at first; I would just accept, accept and accept more and more friend requests. It was not a big deal. I just did it because all of my friends were making such a big deal about it at the time.

I would check my Myspace account every couple of days to look for updates and approve messages being posted on my profile, which consisted mostly of friends and musicians posting banners and pics of events. I became "friends" with some of my favorite musicians and actors, like Alicia Keys (she is hot!), and Kiefer Sutherland (hey, I like 24). I thought ok, Myspace is not that bad. You can connect with a variety of people, from friends to strangers. I was cool with it.

I didn't go crazy over it or anything. One day my account got compromised and someone started to send messages to my friends for advertisements about cell phones and a whole bunch of random nonsense. I was unhappy and eventually closed my account.

Months passed by and the same friends who convinced me to join Myspace told me about Facebook. I was skeptical at first, but again, hopped on the bandwagon. This was a completely different experience. After their initial background check, I was instantly connected with people from as far back as junior high. Some of them even went to my elementary school. All of the connections were completely genuine.

At first it was all about updating my status, sending out wall posts and catching up with long lost friends. I would check their status updates and profiles and see what they were up to. It was great for meet-ups and ad-hoc reunions. At first, I would only check it at night. Then I would start checking it at work or just have it in the background of my other applications. I heard from other friends that some jobs block your access, but not mine. I would be doing my normal work activities and then every once in a while check what's going on in Facebook.

I got into all of the Facebook applications. They were fun and of course time consuming. My favorite of all time was *Mafia Wars*. I think this was the turning point. Mafia Wars was so interactive and all of my friends joined in on the fun. You start off as petty thief, but can work your way up the chain of command by doing jobs and fighting other players.

Facebook became my new pastime. Even though I could view it at work, I still downloaded the Facebook iPhone application. I have never been a smoker, but I would find myself going outside into the breezeway with the rest of the smokers. While they were smoking, I would be on my iPhone navigating through my Facebook account. I didn't think it was serious, I just liked being on Facebook.

My job started to suffer after a while. My tasks were not getting done as promptly as they were previously. The buyer was constantly reprimanding me and questioning my commitment to the store. I lied constantly and told him that my mom was sick. I mentioned that my family is big into email and I'm constantly checking it throughout the day and keeping tabs on the situation.

I think that is when I realized that I had a problem. I never blatantly lied about anything at work before. Maybe little lies like saying that I'm fine when I'm really hung over from the previous night, but nothing major.

The sick mom excuse only lasted for about a month. I just couldn't help myself. I would constantly have to see what everyone was doing on Facebook. I needed to be connected. I must have SNEAKED at least 200 times a day on average. I would either be commenting on someone's status, writing on a wall, uploading a funny picture, commenting on an uploaded picture or just simply changing my status.

It must have been a Friday when my boss called me into his office and talked with me. He was visibly upset and told me to sit down. He said that they do computer audits every once in a while and noticed an unusual amount of time spent on 'www.facebook.com' from my terminal. The old man was clueless about Facebook. He said he mentioned it to his daughter in conversation and she said, "Dad, that's a social networking site my friends and I use to keep up with the latest gossip at school." I guess the fact that his daughter was a teenager and not a full-time employee made him even more annoyed with me. I was fired on the spot.

The funny thing is that my only thought was to update my Facebook status with the following message: "Jeff's boss just gave him a permanent vacation. Who wants to grab drinks?"

I stayed home for the next few weeks on Facebook, night and day. I didn't even watch TV anymore. I would browse news sites every once in a while look-ing for cool things to post in my profile. I stopped going out with my offline friends. It was now strictly about my online friends. They understood me and were there for me 24/7.

I was at the point where I was ignoring my bills. My moment of clarity came when my Internet Service Provider temporarily shut down my connection. I was now without the Internet. I was now without Facebook. My cell phone had been suspended a week prior so I couldn't use my iPhone to gain access to Facebook. I was going crazy without being able to connect to Facebook!

Most of my offline friends were now unavailable and my funds were low so I couldn't afford to get my ISP reinstated. I had to go cold turkey.

I was unresponsive to everything. I felt like there was

a whole other world that I was no longer a part of. I was also getting evicted from my apartment. I was on Facebook so much that I didn't bother looking for another job. I figured one of my online friends may help me, but of course no one did. It was always about their day or just funny jokes.

I ended up moving back to my mother's house. I also came to grips with the fact that I'm a Social Networking Addict and needed help. My mom had a computer and working ISP. Through searching for support groups online, I found www.SocialNetworkingAddiction.com. I have been a member ever since and I'm just taking it one minute at a time. It will take a while to regain the trust of my offline friends and get back into my career, but every day is a new day.

# chapter 3

robert blage

**Real Name: Robert Blage**

**Social Network Name: Robert Blage**

My name is Robert and I'm a Social Networking Addict. My Facebook addiction stemmed out of love. I'm now twenty-six years old. My ex-girlfriend and I were together since I was twenty-one. We broke up last year, but remained online friends. She is with someone else now, but I still check on her through her Facebook page. She has over 400 friends so she never thought to delete me. I don't comment or give her a reason to delete me, but I'm so into her page. I even became friends with some of her new friends so that I can keep track of her wall to wall comments. They easily accept my request because they see that we have at least one mutual friend, which is Cathy, my ex.

I guess I'm a tad bit of an online stalker, but I can't help myself. I'm constantly on her page. It is even to the point that I stopped updating my status. I just want to remain as inconspicuous as possible. I just go to her page and stare at her pictures.

I watch videos that she posted of her and her new boyfriend. She is a Facebook whore herself, so she is constantly updating her profile and albums with fresh content.

Recently, I saw pictures of them on vacation in Jamaica. She looked so cute in her bathing suit. It brought back memories of our Dominican Republic vacation a few years ago. I also keep track of how she is feeling through her status updates. She got promoted and people from work took her out a few weeks ago. I went through the pictures that she took from the bar that they frequent. I guess the trip to Jamaica was a celebratory trip.

I even thought about friend requesting her boyfriend, but decided against it. His name is Paul Carter. Her Relationship Status has that she is in a relationship with Paul Carter. He of course is also tagged in all of her photos. I remember that their relationship status was "It's Complicated" a couple of months ago. I was kind of excited and felt that was my shot to get Cathy back, but two days later a News Feed message stated, "Cathy Duncan went from being 'It's Complicated' to 'In A Relationship.'" I was extremely upset that they made up.

I'm at the point where I am totally hooked on her page. I'm mostly on Facebook to monitor her. I'm not sure if I'm addicted to Facebook or if I'm just using Facebook as a tool to keep track of Cathy. It is not like I wait outside of her apartment or show up at her job. I strictly use Facebook.

I find myself staying home and watching her page all day. If I know that she is going out I eagerly anticipate seeing the pictures she will post from the event. I browse all of her friends' pages that I can access, looking for pictures or anything about Cathy.

I confided in my best friend, Mark, and he suggested that I join www.SocialNetworkingAddiction.com.

# chapter 4

ellen kane

**Real Name: Ellen Kane**

**Social Network Name: Ellen Kane**

My name is Ellen and I'm a Social Networking Addict. I always thought that social networking was normal. It was technology and just another form of communicating with my friends. I admit that I was always on Facebook, but like I said it was just another form of technology, similar to texting or emailing.

My biggest Facebook vice was whacky status updates and having my friends fill in the blanks. I would of course comment on the walls of my friends, but who didn't? I would get thrilled and excited when one of my friends would add a comment to my status updates. It was always about double meanings and making people laugh. If I was having a bad day, I tended to get philosophical. Some of my favorite status updates were:

> "Ellen is sleeping, but NOT ...."
> "Ellen is sometimes never there for ..."
> "Ellen is the meaning, but not the answer"

It got to the point that I was SNEAKING maybe 20 times a day. I would constantly think of status updates. It was my hobby and my guilty pleasure. I was not ashamed nor thought that anything was wrong.

I think that all Social Networking Addicts know when they hit rock bottom. I just couldn't go without checking my Facebook account or SNEAKING. I was previously a smoker and stopped smoking cigarettes. Facebook was so similar to nicotine addiction, especially when I installed the Facebook Blackberry application. I always needed to check or SNEAK. When I was bored I would look at my friends' status updates. It was so addictive. But unlike cigarettes, it was not physically bad for you.

My moment of clarity came after the accident. I was on a highway and driving the speed the limit. I noticed the red message alert light was blinking on my phone and immediately grabbed it to see who might have called. It was a Facebook message; someone posted a comment on my latest status, "Ellen is so OVER ..." It was my friend Kate, her comment was "Jim and you should be." Jim was my ex-boyfriend and we had a bad break-up, but I still loved him. So, of course, I had to laugh at Kate's comment and was attempting to respond when out of nowhere the guy in front of me stopped abruptly. I crashed right into his bumper. I was not wearing my seatbelt, so my head flew into the windshield. There was glass everywhere.

I woke up in the hospital. I was dazed and out of it. The doctor said that I was lucky to be alive. I had a sprained vertebra, a shifted lower disc, and a sprained neck. I also broke my left wrist and sprained my upper right arm from using it to pro-tect my face from the windshield.

I noticed that the EMT guys put my personal be-longings in the room. My phone was still intact and was not in arm's reach. I noticed the light blinking and I couldn't get to it. It drove me crazy that I could not respond and check my Facebook mes-sages. That was when it hit me. I almost died in the accident. I was lying in bed with serious injuries and all that I could think about was my Facebook messages. That was my moment of clarity.

Later on, I asked the nurses to call my mom. She is labeled as "Mom" in my phone and afterwards cut the phone off. I became friends with one of the nurses and confided in her about my Facebook addiction. She told me about a program for Social Networking Addicts that I should look into when I get released. That program was www.SocialNetworkingAddiction.com.

# chapter 5

jennifer towers

**Real Name: Jennifer Towers**

**Social Network Name: Jennifer Towers**

My name is Jennifer and I'm a Social Networking Addict. I was always into taking pictures. Even as a little girl I had a Polaroid camera. I loved it. It was so instantaneous. You point, shoot and show all of your friends the pictures during lunch or after school. Now let's add 10 years to that little girl's age. Also throw in a digital camera, Facebook, and the concept of tagging (facebook functionality where users can link photos to other users). It is so crazy. I tag everything and everyone. I take pictures just to take pictures.

I'm notorious for going to offline social events and taking pictures of everyone. I just capture people for the hell of it. I even take pictures of shoes, tables, hands; basically anything that I can tag. I then post it on Facebook and tag all of my friends. I'm starting to get a lot of negative feedback from them. At first, it was ok, but now, a lot of them say that I'm taking it overboard.

I've been known to take pictures of people and then introduce myself to them. I try to secure their name and email address just so I can find them on Facebook and become their friend so that I can tag them. Nine out of ten times they have no clue who I am. So I always say, "We met last night and I have a picture of you." That is usually a good introduction for them to accept my friend request (a facebook function). Once we become friends, I can check their status updates and frequent places they may go so that I can take more pictures and tag more of their friends.

I have over 1,000 friends and most of them do not know me personally. I met most of them by taking pictures and getting acquainted with them afterwards. If they didn't have a Facebook account, then I would invite them using their email address and would sometimes actually get them to join Facebook. Funny, I should get a job working for Facebook.

I realized that I had a problem recently, when one of my photographs caused a huge personal catastrophe with my best friend Megan. We were all at Corey's house. Corey is our platonic male friend. Corey's friend Jason came over to join us in a night of drinking and watching movies. We were all pretty wasted after we finished the bottle of vodka and drank some beers. I noticed that Jason and Megan were flirting with each other all night. They eventually started to hook up while Corey and I were somewhat passed out. I had to go to the bathroom and on my way back I noticed my camera by my purse. I just couldn't help myself.

I started to snap away. I have a camera that does not make too much noise and has a real subtle flash. These things are useful because I take a lot of pictures and sometimes strangers get mad. So, I got pictures of everyone in the house.

The next day I loaded all of my pictures into Facebook and started my maniac tagging spree. I wanted all of the pictures on Facebook. I ended up tagging Megan and Jason hooking up. I should have stopped myself, but I had to tag all of the pictures. Megan's boyfriend, George, saw the pictures on her profile and broke up with her. I didn't even know that Jason had a girlfriend, but Corey told me that Jason got into a lot of trouble over my tagged pictures.

Megan and I have been friends since my Polaroid days. I'm talking little girls in grade school. She was extremely hurt that I exposed her on Facebook. I tried to convince her that there was no malice on my part. I just had to tag each photo. That was when I realized I had a problem. Who does that? Why couldn't I stop myself? I needed help. I lost a close friend because of that incident and still couldn't stop my picture taking and tagging habits.

Finally, Corey sat me down and said that I needed help. He suggested a group called Social Networking Anonymous or S.N.A. I had no clue what he was talking about. I didn't even know that such groups existed. He said that I could find out more information on www.SocialNetworkingAddiction.com.

# chapter 6

 johnny rocket

**Real Name: Joel Smith**

**Social Network Name: Johnny Rocket**

My name is Joel and I'm a Social Networking Addict. I don't know where to begin. I want to start by saying that I am not a pedophile or some freak. I just like having child friends on the Internet. Most of my online friends are between the ages of 12 and 17. I know a lot of you are judging me, but like I said I'm not some freak. I just think that I relate better to children than adults. I hated my adult network. They always talked about the same thing. On my adult network I was known by my real name, Joel Smith. It was so boring. They posted wall comments about work, how much they hate work, another Monday, TGIF, kids, and blah blah blah. It made me so sick.

I'm 35 and don't really have too much interaction with people under the age of 20. I work as an account manager at a management consultant firm. I spend time with clients and contractors all day. Then I may have some drinks with friends after work. I go to the gym occasionally. Nothing too intense. My life is so boring and average.

I discovered Facebook about a year ago, which was great at first. It added that extra spice to my life. I would now come home and have something to look forward to. I connected with old school friends and some old work colleagues from my previous jobs. After a few months I found myself falling into the same rut of normalcy that plagues my life.

One day while browsing I noticed a comment on my

friend's Paul page. It said, "Uncle Paul I was busy playing Gran Turismo." After reading the message I purchased a PlayStation and Grand Turismo. I had so much fun playing that video game. I have not had that much fun since high school. I would find myself rushing back to my apartment with a new found zest.

After playing the game for a while, I wanted someone to talk with about it, and I also wanted new games. There are forums, but it is a different connection when you have someone in your social networking circle to correspond with about a mutual topic. I thought that my current network would think that I'm strange if I started adding a bunch of 14-year-olds to my network.

I came up with the name Johnny Rocket based on a burger spot. I then created a new profile. I was now 15 year-old Johnny Rocket. I picked some random high school in my city. I then started adding friends. My profile picture was a photograph of a child model that I found browsing the Internet. I filled my profile information with anything that I could find about video games.

The next step was finding friends. I decided to search through Facebook Groups. There were tons of video game groups. These kids were so excited to talk about games and share secrets. Once I established myself to be cool, my friend list started to grow exponentially. In a month, I easily had 500 friends.

I had a good ratio between girls and guys. Some of the girls thought that the picture was cute and friend requested me. Most of the guys were just into the video game talk. I stated that I was an aspiring game designer in the Info section of my profile and that I needed as much practice as possible. So gaming was my life.

I didn't think anything was wrong with my actions. I started to get so engulfed in Facebook. It was amazing and extremely fun to escape from reality with these kids. They were so unlike my adult network. No talk of family, work or anything else that correlates to adulthood. I loved it.

My days consisted of work and rushing home to chat with my kid network. Friends from work convinced me to go drinking. I didn't want to, but they were really on me to come out. I ended up going to the bar with them. That is where I unknowingly met the person that would bring my child social networking adventure to a screeching halt. Her name was Adrienne Smith. I joked and told her that we might be cousins. Smith is of course a common last name and we were totally unrelated.

Adrienne worked at Citibank, which was across the street from my job. She knew one of my colleagues, Jim. During our group conversation, Jim pulled me aside and said that Adrienne was interested in me. Adrienne and I started to exchange small talk over group shots of tequila. She was funny and also very attractive. It was now late and she was about to go home. I offered to wait outside with her until a cab came. While we were waiting for a cab, one thing led to another and we started to kiss. When the cab came we decided to go back to her place. It turned out to be a great night. I couldn't remember the last time I was with a woman. We exchanged numbers and email addresses and I rushed home in the morning so that I could get ready for work.

The next day, I got a call from Adrienne and she said that we urgently needed to talk after work. I was a tad bit worried and wondered what the urgency was about. We met after work at a nearby park. She said instead of emailing me, she decided to add me as a Facebook contact. She figured that everyone has a Facebook account and since we rushed into things she wanted to know more about me. She was surprised that the account that came up was for a 15 year old named Johnny Rocket. That is when my anxiety set in. I must have given her the personal email address that I was so used to using for the last couple of months.

She looked freaked out and asked if I was a pedophile. She threatened to report me and tell the guys at work. That was when I came clean. I told her that I was not a pedophile. I explained everything to her and my new found love for video games. I told her that I know it sounded strange, but I had concrete proof. We went back to my place. I pulled up my laptop and logged into my Johnny Rocket account. I showed all of my correspondence and told her that it was completely innocent. She said that although it was not yet at the pedophile stage, I still needed help. She said that she would not report me and would continue to get to know me if I joined Social Networking Anonymous. She gave me the site www.SocialNetworkingAddiction. com and said that she would join with me as an online friend of a social networking addict.

# chapter 7

michael sandelli

**Real Name: Michael Sandelli**

**Social Network Name: Michael Sandelli**

**FanPage: Michael's Place**

My name is Michael and I'm a Social Networking Addict. The funny thing is that I was really never into the social networking scene. I thought it was huge waste of time. I would hear my friends talk about it and I would ask, "What's the angle, you know the score?" Basically, how can I make money from it? I would just get blank looks. So I just told them to forget about it.

Last year I opened a club. Well, it's really a bar with a small dance area. Sometimes we get some after work parties, but mostly we get locals. It's a comfortable place. My bartender, a sexy young thing, Haley, suggested that I join Facebook and tell my friends about the club. She said that I can also get a Fanpage and get the local members to become fans. She mentioned that it may be a good way to keep people informed of special events. Sounded like a good idea at the time.

At first I was skeptical. I'm 20 years removed from high school and here I get all of these questions about school and work. Ok, I answered them. Then what do you know, I start getting all of these Friend Suggestions. I saw Tony from high school. I haven't seen this guy in 20 years. There was Sarah and Paul. This was like a high school reunion. I ended up seeing all of my old friends from high school and some from middle school. Amazing!!!

We all exchanged pleasantries. People were married. People had kids. The sight of some friends made me want to find others, and so I did. I was actually curious to whatever happened to Gale Bassinni. Gale was my old high school girlfriend. We broke up after high school. She went away to college and I started working at my father's car shop.

I finally found Mikey Number 2 aka Michael Francis. We called him Mikey Number 2 because we were always together and I was physically bigger. So anyway, there was Gale on Mikey's page. Gale was not as slim as I remembered and she was very much married. I friend requested her and then we started to send messages to each other behind the scenes.

Gale was married to a stock broker and had 3 children. She seemed happy. Good for her. I always had a special place in my heart for Gale.

Now back to business. After about 2 weeks of socializing, I almost forgot about the main objective. I looked at other Facebook Fanpages and then set mine up. It was actually cool. Surprisingly some of my friends joined. They must have joined out of support because most of them were not even in the same city as my bar, Michael's Place. I then started a guest list at the bar where my patrons can sign up and leave their email addresses. I sent them all an email with the Facebook Fanpage on the bottom and instructed them to forward to other people in their network.

I racked up around 200 fans of customers, friends and random people. I found myself constantly engulfed in my Fanpage. I was always thinking about how to get more fans for Michael's Place. I started to ask everyone if they would sign up on the Fanpage. Haley told me that customers were starting to complain.

I just couldn't help myself. I felt that everyone who came into the bar should be a Facebook fan of Michael's Place. One day, I took it too far and totally lost it when a customer told me that he did have a Facebook account, but didn't want to become a fan of the bar. He said it was his first time at the bar and he only came because someone invited him. He said that he couldn't become a fan of a place that he does not frequent.

I went nuts. It is one thing if he did not have a Facebook account. But this guy is drinking at the bar and did not want to become a fan of the bar. I was personally insulted. I asked him to leave and take his party with him. That day I lost ten fans from my page and also had to delete some nasty comments. The next day at the bar, Haley suggested that I join Social Networking Anonymous. She said that I could find the site at www.SocialNetworkingAddiction.com.

# chapter 8

**natasha harrington**

**Real Name: Natasha Harrington**

**Social Network Name: Natasha Harrington**

My name is Natasha and I'm a Social Networking Addict. I don't know when it began. I was on Facebook for a while, but I was not a frequent user. I would log on probably once or at most twice a week. I had a pretty active life offline. I had a great career as a branch manager at JPM Chase Bank, a really nice boyfriend, and of course a dog. My boyfriend, Mark, and I would go out maybe three or four times a week. Everything was going well. Facebook was blocked at work so I never logged on during the day, only evenings when I was not busy.

Mark was an accountant, but not a boring one. He was into dining, dancing, exercising and rock climbing on weekends. I was so in love with Mark. He was my world. We were together for about 2 years and I was expecting us to soon get engaged. Mark called me one day at work and told me that he needed to talk with me after work. I really thought that he was about to pop the big question. I immediately called my girlfriend, Sandra, and told her the good news. She told me to hold on. She went to close her office door and then let out a big scream. We were all so very excited. She put me on a conference call with our other girlfriend, Erika, and she had a similar reaction. They were all very happy for me. I could not wait until after work. They of course wanted the play-by-play details of it all.

Mark and I met at our favorite French restaurant, La Sirene. We had a great meal and then Mark started to talk. I thought that this was it. He said that we have been together for two years and he had a great amount of respect for me, which is why he took me to this restaurant. He told me that he does not see us spending the rest of our lives together and that he wanted to break up. I was in total shock! I didn't know what to say or do. I was only able to get one word out, "Why?" He said that he was feeling that way for the last couple of months but thought that those feelings would pass. I immediately thought that there was someone else, but he said there was no one else. He just couldn't see us moving on together.

I spent a couple of weeks in a depressive state. It was horrible. It felt like a dream. I would go to work and come straight home. Sandra and Erika were really there for me, but I was just not over Mark. Sandra is a big fan of Facebook and suggested that I log on and start connecting with old friends. I told her that I'm not looking to get into a relationship. She totally understood and just wanted me to interact more with people.

I took her advice and logged into my account. It felt like ages since I used the application. I started browsing profiles and status updates of my friends. I then started adding my own status updates. For the first week my status updates were things like, "Natasha is Blah," "Natasha is over it," "Natasha is finding Natasha." Some of my friends would then respond with funny comments. It made me feel like I was not alone. I felt like I had a support group.

Facebook soon became part of my daily ritual. I even installed the Facebook application on my Blackberry so that I could stay connected during the day. I was now always on Facebook. I then started to post controversial questions as part of my status update. It was fun. Some of my questions were things like, "If your boyfriend or girlfriend cheated on you, what would you do?" I would get a lot of responses from those types of questions. I felt like a talk show host. It even sometimes helped me get perspective with the Mark situation. For instance I posted, "What are some reasons to end a long term relationship abruptly?"

These questions became a major part of my Facebook activities. I posted about 10 questions a day. Sandra told me to slow down and said that I was SNEAKING. I had no clue what she was talking about. I just knew that I liked thinking of interesting questions and posting it on my status. I would get semi upset when I only received two or three responses. The most responses I ever received were twenty. It was so exciting.

Soon my ten question-a-day habit increased to 30 questions-a-day. I started to miss meetings at work and my performance was slacking. Some people would go outside to smoke a cigarette. I would go out to look at my responses and post new questions on my status.

One day after work Sandra and Erika met me at my house and had what they called "a much needed Facebook intervention." They sat me down and said that I have become an offline introvert since Mark and I broke up. Online I'm an extrovert, but I'm not going out, I rarely talk on the phone, and work is now suffering. As they were talking, I recalled a colleague asking why I missed the last few team drink outings. They told me that it was time to join a website that helped people like me. They told me about Social Networking Anonymous and the online meeting place at www.SocialNetworkingAddiction.com.

# chapter 9

august stone

**Real Name: August Stone**

**Social Network Name: August Stone**

My name is August and I'm a Social Networking Addict. I'm a musician. My music is a cross between Jazz and Neo Soul. I have been a musician all of my life. I'm part of a band. We support ourselves through paid gigs and music sales. Facebook has recently been taking me off my game. We always had a Myspace page where our fans follow us. My social networking activities always consisted of me and the band, never me alone. My new girlfriend, Rachel, suggested that I get a Facebook page because she had one.

I joined Facebook and it was an entirely new world. I lost track of so many friends from high school. After high school I went off and started playing at local bars. Those local bars soon became bars across the country. Now I'm always on the road with my band. It was so great to interact with so many people after 6 years of being out of high school. I just found myself constantly on Facebook. It was amazing.

I later found out about a concept called Facebook groups and I created one called "For People Who Like Jazz." I told my band mates about Facebook, but they told me to leave that crap alone and concentrate on the gigs. From their perspective we had a social networking presence on Myspace for fans and that was good enough.

I didn't bother them about it anymore, but I loved my Facebook group. People left cool comments and uploaded nice pictures of some of the old greats like Miles Davis, Billie Holiday, Ray Charles, Dizzie Gillespie - the list just went on and on. I then decided to create "For People Who Like Neo Soul." Same type of thing. I thought it was so cool, this whole group concept.

I started to create more and more interesting groups. I would then send out constant Facebook emails for people to join the group. As time went on I found myself creating 5 groups a day. I would also manage each and wall post some interesting topics. I would also start discussions on topics pertaining to each group.

On Facebook, time could just fly. My band was getting upset because I would constantly be late to rehearsals. I was always on Facebook. The final straw came when I totally missed a show. I was SNEAKING and heavily involved on my Facebook group pages and lost track of time.

My band mates had a vote and threatened to kick me out of the band if I didn't get my act together. I was devastated because the band was my life before Facebook, but I just couldn't stop SNEAKING on my groups. I turned to Rachel for help. She recommended Social Networking Anonymous and said that I could join their online community located at www.SocialNetworkingAddiction.com.

# chapter 10

fluffy

**Real Name: Zoe Mecklin**

**Social Network Name: Fluffy**

My name is Zoe Mecklin and I'm a Social Networking Addict. The funny thing is that I rarely used my personal profile page on Facebook for myself, it is more so for Fluffy. Fluffy is my beautiful Yorkie, you know, Yorkshire Terrier. She is absolutely FABULOUS. I love Fluffy so much and felt that she needed her own Facebook profile page. All of my friends know Fluffy. I have pictures of Fluffy all around my house. I felt that she needed a wider audience.

About 8 months ago, I created a page for Fluffy. It was so awesome! I took a picture of her wearing a pink shearling coat and used it for a main profile image. It was winter and looked appropriate for the season. I immediately started sending friend requests to all of my friends to add Fluffy to their list.

Some friends thought it was adorable and others thought that it was some kind of joke. Fluffy is kind of feisty so her mood changes constantly throughout the day. I constantly kept her status up to date. Some days it was "Fluffy is hungry," "Fluffy loves her Mama," "Fluffy is going to the park," or "Fluffy feels Absolutely Fabulous."

I found myself updating Fluffy's page at least 25 times a day because her mood changes so much. It is so hard to keep up but I did my best. Like the other day for instance, Fluffy came back from her walk and immediately started barking. She was fine outside. I have no clue what triggered her reaction when we returned home. Regardless, I had to update her status on my Blackberry to "Fluffy just got home and is upset."

My best friends Heather and Susan started to express their concern about my over-involvement with Fluffy's Facebook page. I didn't understand why it was such a big deal. Seriously, both of these bitches loved Fluffy and had no problem with Fluffy when they would come to my house. Why all of a sudden were they concerned about Fluffy's Facebook page? I didn't get it and actually got kind of pissed off about the whole thing.

A few months passed and I was adding new pictures, status updates and even commenting on the walls of my friends as Fluffy. I would do it for hours and hours. Sometimes I'd go until the morning. I started to neglect my offline friends and really became introverted. My best friends once again approached me and said that I was SNEAKING. This time I listened.

I told them that I didn't know how to control myself. Everything was fine before Fluffy's Facebook page. I didn't even notice her drastic mood swings until after I created her Facebook page. It was just so hard to keep up with status updates, but for some reason I felt obligated to. I just had to let everyone know what was going on with Fluffy and that the problem is that her mood changes so much.

The whole thing finally came to a head and I was uncontrollably SNEAKING. I really couldn't stop myself. I reached out to Heather for help. Luckily,

Heather is friends with Bobby, whose sister told him about www.SocialNetworkingAddiction.com. Heather suggested that I join and get a handle of my SNEAKING. I took her advice and here I am.

# chapter 11

**carrie - tyler's mom**

**Real Name: Carrie Reed**

**Social Network Name: Carrie - Tyler's Mom**

My name is Carrie and I'm a Social Networking Addict. I'm in tears blogging this story. Everything feels like a dream, but I can't seem to wake up. I've been in a daze since the incident. My two-year-old son, Tyler, was everything to me. He was my world. The police said that it was not my fault. Social Services did an investigation and found me clear of any potential charges. Even though they said it was not my fault, I really believe that I'm to blame. Tyler was a cute and very happy child. He was so playful. I miss him every day. I let him down. Everyone asked me the same question, "What were you doing when Tyler had the accident?" I was too ashamed to say that I was on Facebook. I was on Facebook SNEAKING while my beautiful baby boy slipped against the table and hit the side of his head against the edge. The doctor said that it was a freak accident and could have happened to any parent. But it didn't happen to any other parent; it happened to me!

I was on Facebook before Tyler was born. During my pregnancy I kept friends informed of what was going on in my tummy. I even posted sonograms of Tyler on my wall. My friends gave me suggestions of names. About two months before he was born I posted on my status update, "Carrie is thinking about names for her son. Any suggestions?"

I received a ton of responses. Some of my friends said, "Jake, Henry, Melvin, Christopher, Jerry, Clifford, Joe, and Frank." My friend, Sally, from high school posted, "Why not Tyler?" I never thought of Tyler, but instantly fell in love with the name. From that day on his name was Tyler.

The pregnancy and delivery was smooth. Tyler was born a nine-pound baby. He was the most adorable little thing. I, of course, took pictures and posted them on Facebook as soon as I was back home from the hospital. Even though I was far away from a lot of my friends, they all felt connected to Tyler. I posted so many pictures of him as he got bigger.

My attention was always on Tyler. I was a good mother. The day of the accident was a normal day, nothing out of the ordinary. Tyler usually woke up early. I heard him and then I woke myself up. I fed him breakfast and we sang songs together. Tyler usually took a nap in the afternoon. While he was napping I was on Facebook catching up with friends. Tyler must have awakened and ran into the living room. The next thing I heard was a thump. He didn't even cry. I immediately ran into the living room. Tyler was on the floor just lying there with a bruise on the right side of his head by his temple. He seemed unconscious. I shook him, but he did not respond. I immediately called 911 and told them what happened. The ambulance came rushing over.

Tyler was pronounced dead when we arrived at the hospital. The doctor said that it was a freak accident. I was in shock. I'm still in shock. That happened last year. I have not been on Facebook since.

# chapter 12

## social networking
## addiction guide

*A Brief Guide To Social Networking Addiction*

## What is Social Networking Addiction?

Social Networking Addiction is a mental illness centered around a dependency of online "FRIENDS" or online interaction on social networks. Social Networking Addicts are unable to control their tendency to be logged in and participating on social networking websites.

## What are some characteristics of Social Networking Addiction?

Some of the most common characteristics of Social Networking Addiction are:

- A feeling that being online is the only way to be noticed by the world at large.
- The longing for another post, update, or chat session (otherwise known as "SNEAKING") before they sleep.
- A strong anticipation to being logged onto their social network of choice and seeing what everyone in their network is doing.
- Episodes of logging onto their social network randomly while in the middle of something completely different.
- Attempts to control their addiction by changing social networks. For example jumping from Myspace to Facebook.
- SNEAKING for long periods of time.
- Deleting wall posts so that others don't notice their excessive amount of posts or updates.

- Binge SNEAKING and sleepless nights due to SNEAKING.
- Drowsiness the next day from long nights of SNEAKING.

## What is S.N.A?

*Social Networking Anonymous* (S.N.A) is an online community of men, women, boys, and girls who help each other control their social networking addiction. They offer support to everyone and anyone who is ready to face their Social Networking Addiction and SNEAKING habits. They all have a unique understanding of each other because people on the site are all social networking addicts, except for the online friends of addicts who join for moral support of a Social Networking Addict.

S.N.A members say that they are currently social networking addicts even when they have not been online for many hours, days, or months. They don't believe that they can be completely free of their addiction because it is literally at their fingertips. Once people have lost the ability to control their SNEAKING, they can never become "former social networking addicts" or "ex-social networking addicts." But in S.N.A, they can become recovering social networking addicts. The community is accessible on www.SocialNetworkingAddiction.com.

## How does S.N.A help the social networking addict?

By participating in an open forum of recovering social networking addicts, new members are encouraged to control their SNEAKING. We believe in the "one minute at a time" concept. Instead of trying to be social networking free forever, Social Networking Addicts concentrate on not SNEAKING at the present moment.

By being offline or not logged onto their social network, newcomers can focus on their offline friend relationships. In order to gain more control of their SNEAKING, we encourage our members to leave their home and participate in offline activities that require limited smart phone access. We also have a guide called "THE 12 STEPS OF SOCIAL NETWORKING ANONYMOUS" that can assist social networking addicts in having happy and useful offline lives.

### What are S.N.A meetings?

Social Networking Anonymous meetings are mostly online at www.SocialNetworkingAddiction.com. Users log on and blog or vlog their stories. Users encourage each other through comment responses and words of advice. The entire premise is to let the social networking addict know that they are not alone. There are also offline meetings where S.N.A members and their online and offline friends can gather and discuss S.N.A related publications like "Facebook Addiction: The Life and Times of Social Networking Addicts."

### Who belongs to S.N.A?

Social Networking Addiction can happen to anyone, similar to other types of illnesses. People of all ages, races, nationalities, religions, cultures, and professions are in S.N.A.

It is not mandatory for S.N.A members to use their real names, so we have no way of keeping an accurate list of members. We maintain an open online community for all of our members, accessible on www.SocialNetworkingAddiction.com.

**Does a social networking addict have to go "all the way down" before S.N.A can help?**

S.N.A was started by a social networking addict, Nnamdi G. Osuagwu, whose SNEAKING became out of control and started to impact other aspects of his life. He felt that others may be going through similar issues. He then carved out a section on his existing web forum, www.IceCreamMelts.com, and dedicated it to all social networking addicts.

**Have any senior citizens joined S.N.A?**

There are all sorts of people in S.N.A. Most S.N.A members are between the ages of 18 and 35, but there are an increasing number of individuals outside of this age range becoming members of S.N.A.

**Who runs S.N.A?**

S.N.A has no real government or social hierarchy. It is hosted by IceCreamMelts.com via Social-NetworkingAddiction.com. The community as a whole is free to work out its own customs and ways of holding meetings. Most meetings are online through the form of blog posts where members encourage and support one another through responses. Some meetings are at offline locations where members meet and discuss topics raised in books on Social Networking Addiction, like the one you are reading. Some meetings take place on a group conference call.

**What does it cost to belong to S.N.A?**

S.N.A is totally free to join and accessible through SocialNetworkingAddiction.com, but funds are definitely needed to keep the online community operating. Members are encouraged to support it by purchasing publications and other products from S.N.A's sponsor, Ice Cream Melts, LLC (www.IceCreamMelts.com).

**What can the friends of social networking addicts do?**

S.N.A is for everyone. Friends can log onto SocialNetworkingAddiction.com and support their online and offline friends.

**What does S.N.A NOT do?**

- S.N.A does NOT have a lot of rules.
- S.N.A does NOT accept money outside of ad revenue and product purchases.
- S.N.A does NOT prevent social networking addicts and their friends from logging onto SocialNetworkingAddiction.com.

- S.N.A does NOT provide laptops, smart phones, or other such devices to their members.
- S.N.A does NOT monitor or check up on its members. It empowers social networking addicts to help themselves and control their SNEAKING.
- S.N.A does NOT connect members of the community for the formation of online friendships.

**How can you find out more about S.N.A?**

Find out more about S.N.A by visiting www.Social-NetworkingAddiction.com or its sponsor, www.IceCreamMelts.com.

# chapter 13

## social networking anonymous 12 Steps

## THE 12 STEPS OF SOCIAL NETWORKING ANONYMOUS

1. We came face to face with our online social networking addiction.
2. We came to believe that there is more to life than our online community.
3. We made a decision to reconnect with our offline community.
4. We self assessed our situation with complete honesty.
5. We admitted to our online friends that we were SNEAKING way too much.
6. We will deactivate our social networking profile if that becomes the last resort.
7. We will be courteous to our Internet Service Provider when disrupted Internet connections prevent us from going online.
8. We made a list of online friends whom we have spammed by constantly SNEAKING and apologized for our actions.
9. We apologized to our offline friends whom we have ignored due to continuous SNEAKING.
10. We continue to self assess our situation and admit when we are SNEAKING.
11. By engaging in offline activities we are adding more to our lives and learning to cope in a world outside of our online social network.
12. We seek to continuously gain a higher understanding of our social networking addiction and spread the word to other social networking addicts in our offline and online interactions.

# chapter 14

## basic structure of social networking anonymous

**BASIC STRUCTURE OF SOCIAL NETWORKING ANONYMOUS**

1. Our Social Networking Recovery depends on the unity of the online community at www.SocialNetworkingAddiction.com.
2. There is no hierarchy in our group: everyone can contribute and be heard.
3. S.N.A is a group formed by Social Networking Addicts and friends of Social Networking Addicts.
4. There are different S.N.A groups, which are all connected on www.SocialNetworkingAddiction.com.
5. The primary goal of the community is to get social networking addicts to come to grips with their addiction.
6. The community shall be kept free of charge and accessible to all.
7. The S.N.A group will encourage members and friends of members to purchase S.N.A related publications.
8. Social Networking Anonymous shall be free of politics.
9. S.N.A can create sub-communities in other forums to reach more social networking addicts.
10. Social Networking Anonymous shall avoid taking a stance on external issues.
11. S.N.A has a very open public relations policy and does NOT shy away from the press, radio or films.
12. The online community at www.SocialNetworkingAddiction.com shall always be a place where all can come and share their stories through blogs or vlogs.

# chapter 15

## social network addiction
## childhood theory

There is a new theory that suggests that some people may be predisposed to Social Networking Addiction based on childhood influences. Children from large families who took part in continuous family gatherings could have a predisposition to the idea of staying connected. Usually in such households, family gatherings also included a subset of family friends. As the child grew up, he or she witnessed their family spread apart and become less connected. At times these tight knit groups broke up into subsets and such large gatherings were not common place anymore. As the child grew older and left home, they lost more of a connection with their once tight knit circle of relatives and family friends.

When that child is exposed to an online social network as an adult, they tend to hold onto their online friends and psychologically place an extraordinarily high value on those connections.

Let's take the example of a Social Networking Anonymous Member, whom we'll call "Damien." Damien's nuclear family immigrated to New York City from Jamaica in 1991 when Damien was 4 years old. His nuclear family consisted of his sister, mother and father. The family lived in Damien's uncle's house for their first 5 years in New York. During that time the house was packed, they were constantly surrounded by cousins and family friends who came to visit. Holidays, although crowded, were filled with laughter and love. In 1996 Damien's father got a job opportunity in Allentown, PA. The family ended up moving to Allentown and purchasing their first home. Even though it was a lucrative opportunity and good for the family, everyone was pretty sad about the move.

As the years passed, the entire family got together more and more infrequently. The relatives in New York would only come to Allentown on special occasions. Damien's nuclear family would only visit New York on certain holidays. Eventually through local organizations, like church groups, Damien's family fostered new relationships in Allentown.

Damien eventually went away to college. Once again, although it was a good opportunity, this meant another move in Damien's life. Subconsciously he always felt like he was losing touch with the people who were close to him. During his time in college, he formed new relationships and found a way to fit in.

Damien was introduced to Facebook while in college and immediately gravitated towards the idea of keeping his circle of friends close. He spent a lot of time on Facebook and formed friend connections with people he hardly knew. His online community of friends became the most important thing to him because it represented stability.

There were times when Damien would SNEAK for hours throughout the day and night. He was seriously slacking on his studies due his social networking addiction. Damien sought help when he realized that he was about to flunk out of school. That is when Damien joined *Social Networking Anonymous.*

We can say that in Damien's case, constant childhood relocations caused a deep psychological need to stay connected to friends and family. Once he was introduced to Facebook that need took center stage and Damien became mentally dependent on his social network. Maybe if Damien was not constantly uprooted as a child he might not have been hypersensitive to Social Networking Addiction.

Damien's case is one of many. Many psychologists are pondering over this new phenomenon, which has many names: Facebook Addiction, Internet Addiction and of course Social Networking Addiction.

The following chapter contains news articles that support this theory.

# chapter 16

## news articles

**The following articles in this chapter were extracted from the New York Daily News:**

**Facebook status update becomes suicide note for aspiring Brooklyn model, actor Paul Zolezzi**

An aspiring model tormented by heroin addiction hanged himself in a Brooklyn playground early Friday after foretelling his suicide on Facebook.

A jogger discovered the body of Paul Zolezzi, 30, dangling from the monkey bars in Mount Prospect Park playground near the Brooklyn Museum about 7a.m., police said.

Hours earlier, Zolezzi had updated his Facebook page with an apparent suicide note, saying he was "born in San Francisco, became a shooting star over everywhere, and ended his life in Brooklyn. ... And couldn't have asked for more."

Zolezzi's mother, Stephanie Zolezzi, told the Daily News her son had been in a downward spiral since a broken engagement two years ago.

"I would say that people get so lonely, so delusional, that all they want to do is be remembered," she said from her home near San Francisco.

"He probably wanted to be remembered in a big way, to do it dramatically. That's what drugs will do to people."

She said her son - who had tried acting and modeling with little success - was busted in San Francisco last fall for buying heroin and skipped town.

He stayed in Portland, Ore., and then 10 days ago came to Brooklyn, where he had lived before. He crashed on the couch of friend Melissa Lopez, who said she was disturbed by his "dark" behavior.

"I think he was really sick," Lopez, 33, said, explaining Zolezzi had been talking to himself. "But I was in shock because you never think somebody is going to go that far."

Zolezzi's father, a schizophrenic writer, threw himself off the Golden Gate Bridge in his 40s, so his mother worried about her son's mental state and drug use.

She tried to get him to check into a Christian drug rehab center, but he balked. She had not seen him since September and didn't know he was in New York until police called after finding her number in his cell phone.

"I didn't know what was going on in his life. All I knew is that he knew I was always trying to pray for him," Stephanie Zolezzi said. "He needed an adjustment to his ego. He couldn't give up the fantasies about what he wanted his life to be."

Her son broadcast some of his disillusionment on Facebook in what the social-networking site refers to as "status updates" - short messages that can be seen by other users.

"Paul is wondering, what unspeakable act did I do in a previous life to deserve this one?" he wrote in late January.

"Paul is going to be the first person ever to hang himself on the way out of Portland! Everything here sucks!" he wrote just before coming to New York.

The page was apparently pulled down last night.

After he updated his status for the last time at 8:40 p.m. Friday, a clueless buddy apparently couldn't tell if he was joking about ending his life.

"Are you dying? or just staying brooklyn?" the friend commented on his Facebook page. "I hope its the latter."

## Social networking makes massive gains in Americans' time

The nightclub and the coffee shop are no longer the kingdoms of the social scene.

A new Nielsen Online report says Americans spend 83% more time on social networking and blog Web sites than in 2008.

Facebook replaced MySpace as the most frequented social networking site in terms of total minutes used. The new No. 1 saw a 700% increase in member usage, soaring to 13.9 billion April 2009 from 1.7 billion minutes used in April 2008.

Michael Lawrence, 49, of Hell's Kitchen, credits Facebook's success to user-friendly features.

"I've actually been able to find people from many years ago who I had no way of contacting," he said.

**EMT that posted photo of murdered woman on Facebook charged with official misconduct**

A snap-happy paramedic was charged with official misconduct for taking a photo of a murdered woman and posting the image on his Facebook page, authorities said Wednesday.

Mark Musarella, 46, took the picture of Caroline Wimmer, who was found strangled with a hair dryer cord on Mar. 30 in her Staten Island apartment.

The ghoulish EMT later then put the pic online, his lawyer admits, insisting it was a mistake.

"It is unconscionable to me that an EMT . . . would take a photo of a murder victim and post it on the Internet for all to see," said Staten Island District Attorney Daniel Donovan.

Musarella, a retired NYPD detective, was fired from his job at Richmond University Medical Center. He faces up to a year in prison.

His lawyer said he was only "following his instincts" in using his cell phone to snap a photo of Wimmer's lifeless body and insisted he never meant to post it.

"Mr. Musarella is deeply sorrow [sic] for any pain this incident has caused," said Edward Pavia, the lawyer. "He never intended for the photo to be displayed."

Police said Calvin Lawson, 28, killed Wimmer, 26, because she told his girlfriend that he was unfaithful. Lawson has been charged with murder and possession of a weapon.

**Facebook members with hundreds of online friends only have a few 'true' friends**

If you have hundreds of friends, doesn't it mean that your social calendar is brimming with engagements? That you're out and about almost every night of the week?

Not necessarily, especially if those friends are just 'Facebook friends.'

The Daily Mail reports the following:

A new study finds that even though the average user of Facebook has a network of 100 friends, he or she regularly keeps in contact with only a few of them.

Men who have 500 online friends regularly keep in touch with ten of them, women with sixteen of them. Men with 120 friends on Facebook only keep in regular contact with four, women with six.

The Economist states: 'Humans may be advertising themselves more efficiently. But they still have the same small circles of intimacy as ever.' The other hundreds of friends within a person's Facebook network are usually only acquaintances.

So, while the Facebook generation seems to have many more acquaintances than older generations, its core group of 'true' friends is about the same size.

Many experts conclude that Facebook users and members of other social networking sites are merely 'broadcasting their lives to an outer tier of acquaintances,' rather than making true relationships.

## Prominent politician posts picture of herself in shower on Facebook

Sure politics can be seedy. Spitzer and his prostitute, Clinton and his affair, and the list goes on. But usually, politicians are at least trying to keep their scandalous behavior under wraps.

Well, maybe not Uruguay's interior minister, Daisy Tourne.

On her Facebook page, Tourne, 57, published a photo of herself in the shower above the caption, "there's nothing more natural than a woman in the shower," according to El Pais, Montevideo newspaper (as reported by The Telegraph).

Now, it's not full nudity. It only shows her face and hands amidst running water in the shower. But still, a national leader with a shower photo - it's creating some controversy.

Opposition leaders have called her "an exhibi- tionist," the Telegraph reports.

"I think it's in very bad taste that the minister exposes herself so intimately," former Vice President Luis Hierro Lopez told El Pais (as re- ported in The Telegraph). "Ministers have to be more austere, modest — above all the Minister of the Interior."

Tourne said the photograph was not supposed

to be erotic. She claims it was taken when she was rinsing off after a day at the beach, El Pais reported.

Facebook is a social networking site with more than 130 million users worldwide.

**The 'world's first divorce by Facebook'**

Facebook has taken relationships to a new level.

You can secretly look at pictures of your ex on it. You can even look at his/her new significant other if you guys are "friends." And so much more. But Emma Brady's relationship nightmare takes the Facebook relationship dynamic to a whole new level.

Emma Brady will be getting the "world's first divorce by Facebook," according to the Daily Mail.

The Daily Mail also reported:

Brady, a 35-year-old conference organizer, claims that she found out that her husband wanted a divorce via Facebook. She said her friend was looking at Facebook and discovered that Brady's husband, a 39-year-old IT consultant, had posted this message: "Neil Brady has ended his marriage to Emma Brady."

And it gets worse: Emma said that she then saw a message from someone else that stated that Neil was "better off out of it."

'I only joined Facebook because the girls at work said it was good fun. What upset me the most was not the fact that Neil had written he had ended his marriage, but the comment from a girl in Canada who said: "You are better off out of it". It hurt me that he had been speaking to someone else about it,' Emma Brady told the Daily Mail.

Emma alleges that even after Neil posted that message, he still didn't tell her for a while that he wanted a divorce.

'He acted like everything was fine so we carried on as normal,' she told the Daily Mail.

Neil Brady said he did tell his wife about wanting to leave her, stating, 'I'd had enough of her.'

He now lives with his mother.

# chapter 17

## conclusion

Thanks for taking this journey through a tale of fictional reality. The goal of this book was to show a real parallelism between online addiction and chemical addiction. Although this book is fictional, the characters described do mirror real life circumstances. Research has also shown that some individuals are dependent and self-proclaimed addicts to their online social networking communities.

Please note that all aspects of this book, EXCEPT for the actual news articles, are fictitious. The website www.SocialNetworkingAddiction.com is REAL, but is based on the book that you've just read. We encourage our readers to log onto the site and share their personal Social Networking Addiction stories and comment on our blogs. We also encourage our readers to post videos on the site as well. All books published by Ice Cream Melts Publishing are interactive and engage our readers both online and offline.

It is important to note the following chapters:

Chapter 11.   Social Networking Addiction Guide
Chapter 12.   Social Networking Anonymous 12 Steps
Chapter 13.   Basic Structure of Social Networking Addiction

The concept of the above chapters was derived from documents found from Alcoholics Anonymous. This book is in no way making light of Alcoholics Anonymous. Ice Cream Melts Publishing commends the bravery of the individuals who decided to join such organizations and seek help for their addictions. We have also blogged and video streamed the courageous stories of A.A members for the "What's Your Ice Cream Melts Story?" online project.

People who are displaying signs of Social Networking Addiction are encouraged to get out more and spend time doing things offline. Staying connected with friends is a beautiful thing, but like all indulgences, moderation is key ....

social networking
 terms and definitions

**Bebo:** Online social networking website, which can be found at http://www.bebo.com.

**Facebook:** Online social networking website, which can be found at http://www.facebook.com.

**Facebook Addict:** someone who is constantly SNEAKING on Facebook.

**Facebook Fanpage:** Facebook functionality which enables a user to form an alternate page that other users can join as fans.

**Facebook Groups:** Facebook functionality where different users can come together around a particular topic or issue.

**Facebook Intervention:** Offline friends getting together to help a Facebook Addict.

**Flickr:** Online photo sharing website, which can be found at http://www.flikr.com.

**Friend Request:** Facebook functionality where users can invite other users into their online social network.

**Friend Suggestion:** Facebook functionality where users can suggest friends to other users in their network.

**Myspace:** Online social networking website, which can be found at http://www.myspace.com.

**News Feed:** Facebook functionality that displays

updated information about people in your online social network.

**Offline Friends:** People that you know outside of your online social network. Online Friends can also be Offline Friends.

**Online Friends:** People listed on your social networking website community as friends.

**Post:** Facebook functionality which means to write a message.

**Profile:** a user's personal space which displays information about the user.

**Relationship Status:** Facebook functionality where the user can provide their current romantic situation.

**SNEAKING:** Anything pertaining to activities on your favorite social networking website. Examples are wall posts, status updates, commenting on pictures, etc.

**Social Networking Addiction:** Having a psychological dependency on your online social networking community.

**Social Networking Anonymous:** Online group formed to help Social Networking Addicts.

**Status:** Facebook functionality where users can write messages pertaining to their current activity, which will appear on their page.

**Tagging:** Facebook functionality where users can link photos, videos, and notes to other users.

**Twitter:** Online social networking website where users send short status updates, which can be found at http://www.twitter.com.

**Wall Post:** Facebook functionality where users can write messages on the pages of their friends.

# references

Alcoholics Anonymous World Services, Inc. (1972). A Brief Guide To Alcoholics Anonymous. Retrieved March 11, 2009, from Alcoholics Anonymous: http://www.aa.org/lang/en/catalog.cfm?orig-page=18&product=8

New York Daily News Articles:

©NY Daily News, L.P., used with permission

Gendar, A., & Connor, T. (2009, February 20). Facebook status update becomes suicide note for aspiring Brooklyn model, actor Paul Zolezzi. Retrieved April 7, 2009, from NY Daily News: http://www.nydailynews.com/news/2009/02/20/2009-02-20_facebook_status_update_becomes_suicide_n.html

Michael, R. (2009, June 04). Social networking makes massive gains in Americans' time Retrieved June 11, 2009, from NY Daily News: http://www.nydailynews.com/lifestyle/2009/06/04/2009-06-04_webs_hotspot_for_socializing.html

Goldiner, D. (2009, June 04). EMT that posted photo of murdered woman on Facebook charged with official misconduct. Retrieved June 11, 2009, from NY Daily News: http://www.nydailynews.com/news/ny_crime/2009/06/04/2009-06-04_emt_that_posted_photo_of_murdered_woman_on_facebook_charged_with_official_miscon.html

Catey, H. (2009, March 02). Facebook members with hundreds of online friends only have a few 'true' friends. Retrieved June 11, 2009, from NY Daily News: http://www.nydailynews.com/money/2009/03/02/2009-03-02_facebook_members_with_hundreds_of_online-1.html

Catey, H. (2009, January 19). Prominent politician posts picture of herself in shower on Facebook. Retrieved June 11, 2009, from NY Daily News: http://www.nydailynews.com/money/2009/01/19/2009-01-19_prominent_politician_posts_picture_of_he.html

Catey, H. (2009, February 06). The 'world's first divorce by Facebook.' Retrieved June 11, 2009, from NY Daily News: http://www.nydailynews.com/money/2009/02/06/2009-02-06_the_worlds_first_divorce_by_facebook.html

keep in touch

# let's keep in touch

What's your Social Networking Addiction?

We are interested in hearing about your social networking addiction and general thoughts about the book.

Please visit **http://www.TheFacebookAddiction.com**, blog in your story, upload pictures if available, join ongoing blog discussions, or just share your thoughts about the book.

If you have friends that are Facebook Addicts and feel that this book can be beneficial, take part in their Recovery Program and purchase this book at a wholesale price when you buy 10 or more copies. **http://www. TheFacebookAddiction.com/wholesale**

Please send all inquiries to **info@IceCreamMelts. com**.

# acknowledgements

# acknowledgements

I would like to thank the following people for their participation in the Audio version of this book:

David "Traum Diggs" Shanks
Michelle Gonzalez
Andrea Donkor
Rhowshad Hammonds
Randy Tonge
Keah Buck

Thanks to all of my friends and family who reviewed this book during the infant stages. Just to name few:

Sonia Butler Canzater
Emeka Osuagwu
Renee Brown
Tunmise Awojobi
Jennifer Glover

Thanks to the Ice Cream Melts team for keeping up with the vision of making our books interactive with accompanying online blog and video components. You guys ROCK !!!

Nathaniel Thomas
Prabhat  Sandheliya

Special thanks to the Outskirts Press team for putting this project together, especially:

Jennifer Jensen
Wendy Stetina

Last, but not least, I would like to thank the wonderful team at Facebook for making such a brilliant product. As a computer science major, I have the utmost appreciation for your application.